Truth
Love
&
Simplicity

Copyright © 2010 Kevin Wright
All rights reserved.

ISBN: 1452849331
ISBN-13: 9781452849331

Edited by
Trish Knudsen

Designed by
Ismat Rahman

Illustration by
Sandy Gibson
www.pbase.com/sandygibson

Also By Kevin Wright

Far from Home
Pieces to a Dream
It was Written

Truth Love & Simplicity

Kevin Wright

Truth Love and Simplicity: because love needs truth and simplicity follows.

This is for love and everything that it has brought me through greatness, truth, love, and simplicity. I thank you from the depths of my soul for breathing new life into my lungs.

Acknowledgements

I would like to thank Destiny, who is my guiding light in the sky.

CONFESSION

WHEN I STARTED OUT WITH THIS PEN THAT NEVER LEFT MY SIDE, IT LEAD ME INTO THE SKY, AND I BEGAN TO CREATE THE THOUGHTS I WAS HAVING IN WHAT I CALLED REALITY. I STARTED TO LISTEN TO MUSIC AND MAKE SENSE OF IT, MUSIC CONVERTED INTO LOVE. I WAS INFATUATED WITH IT. I STARTED OUT THAT MORNING AT A COFFEE SHOP, SIPPING ON A HOT CHOCOLATE MOCHA, SIZE VENTE. I BEGAN TO WRITE, AND WRITE, AND WRITE. I WAS THINKING OF LOVE, A LOVE REBORN. THE FIRE IGNITED AGAIN; IT BEGAN TO BURN TILL I COULDN'T WITHSTAND THE HEAT. I TOLD LOVE I KNEW HER REALLY EARLY. THE WORDS BEGAN TO FLOW; I WANTED TO WRITE A BOOK ABOUT LOVE AND WHAT SHE HAS DONE TO ME UP TO THIS POINT. I CAN ONLY SIT BACK AND WONDER IF LOVE IS GOING TO TAKE ME TO THE PROMISED LAND. TRUTH BE TOLD, I WILL BE THE ONE TO TAKE DESTINY ON A JOURNEY TO PLACES IN MY HEART NO ONE HAS EVER BEEN. I DEDICATE THIS BOOK TO LOVE; I WILL LOVE HER FOR LIFE. THE ONE I WILL NEVER BETRAY, AND LOVE TO MAKE SMILE; THE SUN SHINES ON YOUR BEAUTIFUL HEART. I WILL AWAKE TO ITS BEAT AND OPEN ARMS.

"I fell in love again in a coffee shop" -- *Kevin Wright*

Live as if you were to die tomorrow. Learn as if you were to live forever. --*Gandhi*

Life is like riding a bicycle. You don't fall off unless you plan to stop peddling. -- *Claude Pepper*

In the game of life it's a good idea to have a few early losses, which relieves you of the pressure of trying to maintain an undefeated season. -- *Bill Baughan*

It is not length of life, but depth of life.
-- *Ralph Waldo Emerson*

To Love:

To love this book was built on emotion and passion to express the desire that I feel for you. The entirety of your existence, your smile, your courage, the way you hold me, the way you kiss me. The feeling you give me, the meaning you give to me, I love you love. Thank you for being my shade, my sunshine, my dark nights, my morning sunshine, brightest at midday. Love, thank you.

To my friends and family

Marco, I stay patiently waiting for your book to come in the mail. To my family, I love you and God bless. To my friends, I hope I give you something to look forward to as well as fresh air to this thing we call life. Thank you all and much love from the bottom of my heart.

To Truth:

Thank you for leading me astray and taking me back up and around the corner. You led me to love and what it meant, its lies and deceit, its undying passion to want to create a love forevermore. Thank you truth for giving me that feeling of hope, and truthfulness, your words, your words are uncanny I must say. Truth you led me to love, I thank you.

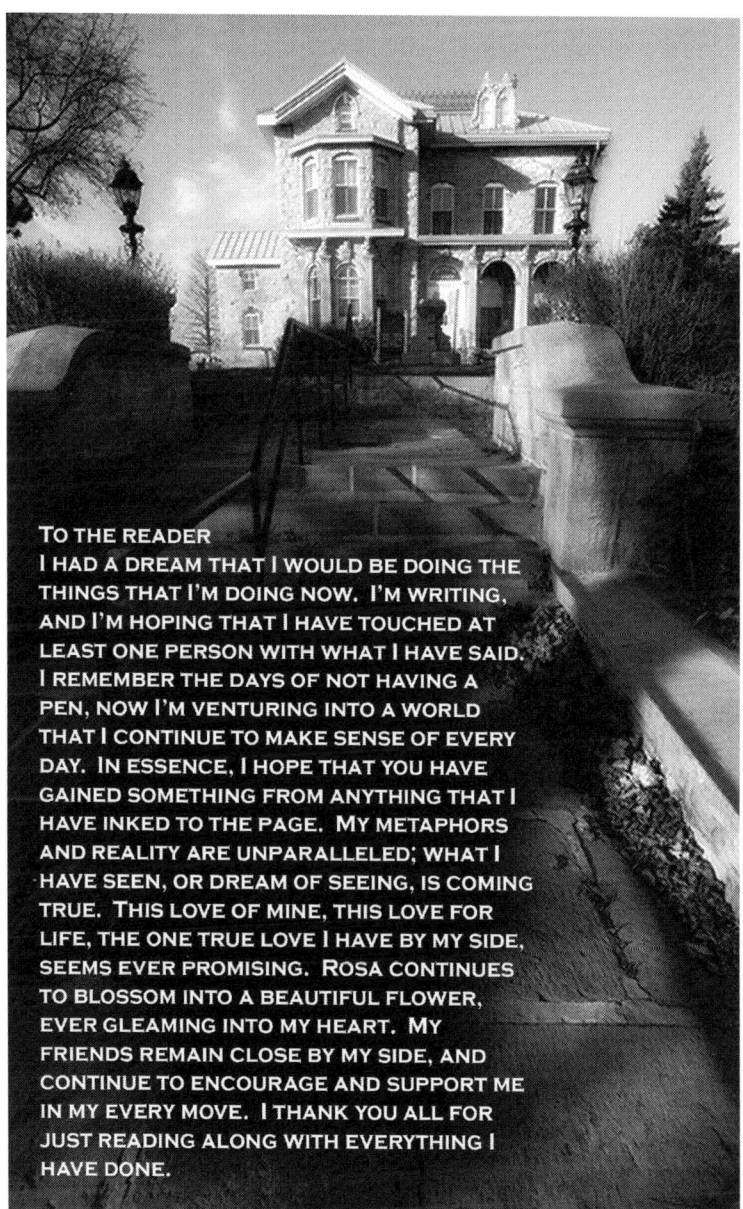

TO THE READER
I HAD A DREAM THAT I WOULD BE DOING THE THINGS THAT I'M DOING NOW. I'M WRITING, AND I'M HOPING THAT I HAVE TOUCHED AT LEAST ONE PERSON WITH WHAT I HAVE SAID. I REMEMBER THE DAYS OF NOT HAVING A PEN, NOW I'M VENTURING INTO A WORLD THAT I CONTINUE TO MAKE SENSE OF EVERY DAY. IN ESSENCE, I HOPE THAT YOU HAVE GAINED SOMETHING FROM ANYTHING THAT I HAVE INKED TO THE PAGE. MY METAPHORS AND REALITY ARE UNPARALLELED; WHAT I HAVE SEEN, OR DREAM OF SEEING, IS COMING TRUE. THIS LOVE OF MINE, THIS LOVE FOR LIFE, THE ONE TRUE LOVE I HAVE BY MY SIDE, SEEMS EVER PROMISING. ROSA CONTINUES TO BLOSSOM INTO A BEAUTIFUL FLOWER, EVER GLEAMING INTO MY HEART. MY FRIENDS REMAIN CLOSE BY MY SIDE, AND CONTINUE TO ENCOURAGE AND SUPPORT ME IN MY EVERY MOVE. I THANK YOU ALL FOR JUST READING ALONG WITH EVERYTHING I HAVE DONE.

To Simplicity:

Thank you for your ease to love and everything that walks with me. The knack I have for you is unlike any other, I love what I have, and what it's taking me to get to that destination.

First and foremost, this book is for love and everything it has brought me. I'd like to thank my family and friends for their continuous support over the years and the love they have shown me, for if it wasn't for them, I wouldn't still have this ink flowing. I'd like to thank Trish for putting up with my outrageous demands, and simply just being an amazing person and friend. I would like to thank Hayden for giving me thought; Marco for giving me reason and for that the solution I derived to, which these books have brought to life. You may not know, but you have been such an integral part of what keeps me going. I would like to also thank Sandy Gibson for providing the artwork which brought this book to life. To Ismat, for being a part of my grind, and riding this wave with me once again. S.B. this is just another classic to be a part of, after 9 shots we're still here, ringing in another day. God bless my nephews. Tamar you have been everything and more, and I thank you for everything. Rosa Marchese, thanks for being a part of such a important journey, from the cave to the sunlight where salt water exists. We swung on the rainbows where no one saw us, we climbed heights to which we never thought to reach, and for that I thank you. Live, laugh, love. To Marianne, thanks for that push and drive to search for more with this ink. To Julia Carter, I have said it before, and I'll say it again, you are my inspiration. Through it all you have always stuck by me. To my friend Bisi what more can i say about you that I love you and you have been their since day one. To my friend TT I'm always here through the fighting and fussing. To my God daughter, Nai, I love you and I'll always be there for you. Zee, what can I say about you? You have always brought me back to life with just being that person I needed to stay sane; for that I thank you. As my great friend said once before, if the cookie is meant to crumble it will, and that's that. Amanda Costa I love you your amazing, Sasha, Krystina, Shawna, Sameena, Nicole, Laura, Anne, Melissa, Ashley Johnson, Keith Johnson, Vanessa, Naida, Ash, Tarika, and Krystal to name a few; I thank you all, for everything. Love live life xo.

Lost thoughts and placated dreams
The tears have me jaded
Tomorrow is not forgotten
For it is not here
Today is today
Yesterday is not a distant memory
Life takes its place
As the clouds move out of place
Sense is not cents
Rather inklings of nature
Forgive the innocence
For life is life
Love is love
The words they write
I am not them

When she comes knocking
Let her in
She speaks of good wisdom
Her love is sincere
Her words sweat you
Draining from your scalp
Down your back
As you speak through the peep hole
Look and stare
Watch how love shines
Look with both eyes
No squinting involved
She appears at birds' eye view
Assemble your thoughts
Turn the lock
Open slowly
As the light shines ever so bright
Let love in
Love at your doorstep

They meant well I assume
Though I don't belong
The rules of engagement changed
I can still ride the bus
Back or front
Cross the street
The colour of my skin has a recollection
I haven't escaped the biases
I know not my past
Nor do I pretend to
I neglect to mention my thoughts much
Just the thoughts that reflect my current state
Current state of position
State of mind
My color
My race
Culture has its bias
I am what you see
Create your own bias

I question whether I'm free
What Martin meant to me
What Rosa did for my people
What Malcolm said
Whether my words are of significance
What Nikki Giovanni said to me
Her words and what they speak of
The genius she is
Her witty thoughts
I wonder if she'll ever read this
Nikki if you're listening
Thank you
Simply for your words

They think I don't sleep enough
I am drained mentally
How do I have these thoughts?
Love is a beautiful thing
Life is beautiful
Dreams of Milo have me reaching
The stars sleep to my calm heartbeat
If you wonder how I do it
This is how I get it done

As I play with the words that come to mind
As they try to escape the coffee shop
The next mixture in your latte
The sugar in your tea
The extra shot of mocha
You already have three
Don't be greedy, you can read too
Just as soon as I'm done
They will see why I do this

It can rain non-stop
Love can be the same way
It trickles down your cheek
As rain trickles down the window
The cars drive by as people walk by
I wonder, do they know
Know about why they're here
What it means to be a part of the world
The beauty of the stop sign
The hazardous lights that flicker
I'm not sure if they think so deeply
As my thoughts wander
I wonder if theirs do as well

I love you for giving me new life
You made me want to love you
I love you more than I love life
I love the change you created
I saw you that Sunday morning and your smile
I decided I never wanted to love you
You decided my fate
I love you
Because you loved me

They say the lord will work it out
His words hold significance
I wonder if he speaks for me
He doesn't, does he?
I think he can hear my words
My thoughts bleed internally
The expressions on my face
Tell a different story
I'm sure he can read the words on my kite
As I sit in the clouds

Africa tells me a story
Insistent are the distant thoughts
The words write to me
I write to me
Speaking of what, I do not know
From what I think I know
Confused are the words as I tell my story
What is your story?

I wonder if you called out to me
I've been too long on my own
I fell deep in that tunnel
Sunlight never came by
Night was my every day
Darkness kept me at that hump
That spark was dead
The switch was left out
Bulbs missing the wire
No shock
I was never in shock
This was my position
Today and yesterday
Perhaps tomorrow will be different
Love awaits, maybe at my door
In my dreams, she knocked
In my reality, love appeared
Rose in hand

Never for I will be there
When your eyes close
When they re-open
My lips await your presence
Sleep my love
Love sleep

Up the rainbow
Down the other side
My heart sits
Anxiously awaiting you
To come down the other side
For your side was my side,
My side of love
The music of love
Sings to your soul
Your heart says forever more
My love beyond eternity
The birds and bees sing
At your bedside
Morning, noon and night

Vacation time
I have yet to see the sunset in beautiful Italy
I hear the wine is quite the delight
Dreams have me unfulfilled
Moments in mind have me convinced
I am not where I want to be
Elsewhere from home
Captivates my existence
For my heart is distant
I move to its beat
As they pour the wine
I search for sound
Pouring into tall and skinny glasses
I wait to sip love
Love is elsewhere
Not here

Relevance is key
The chapters have no place
The words leave not a mark
The substance has weight
The health standard is high
The brain power is deep
Food for thought
I am a breath of fresh air

I write what I see
I write what I be
I create the sites to see
I am the writing on the wall
I wrote it
Spit on it called it mine
I bashed it and fell in love
I forgave it
These were my thoughts
I was mad
I cried and smiled
More so, I loved it
Cherishing it
Sense was everything
Scent was where it began

My pen left the page
Thoughts came to mind
Never finding my way back
Home was my last option
Far away was possible
Far away
Far far away
I left a lot to be written
A lot to be said
I remained mute
The button stalled
I stayed down in the elevator
My words never arose
Love seems to slowly come back
Again and again

Michael Jackson healed the world
First man to moonwalk on the moon
He graced us with his presence
He was chosen from the stars
Unique he was in charisma
His tenacity
The money wasn't his
He gave it to the sky
Africa knows, as does the world
I looked in the sky this morning
I asked you why you left
You replied, son don't let go
Let your words speak
Speak to whoever listens
If they don't continue to impound the thoughts
My music will live on
Your words are empowering my son
I looked back to the stars
Hovering over me
I replied
Thank you

Love's resistance is its existence
Resist relinquishing
The threshold is not minor, rather awkward
Painless is the hurt
For the heart has left nothing behind
A battered child
Lost father to guide
For he has no pride
His departure was not denied
Feelings tell a tale
In that Holy Grail
For God he must answer to
Her father will always remain
Remain in the sky
Clouds hovered
While darkness placates the city

I can stand or sit
Walk and let my eyes wonder
They witnessed segregation
Struggled for 300 years
Martin spoke for me
Rosa walked for me
Malcolm gave me the speed to run
Obama came to me
Son you can fly

Inspiration is such a creeper
The thoughts are sporadic
I remain the best kept secret
My words so silent
Reaching few ear drums
I beat the blocks
Quietly they can hear my footsteps
I cross the minds
Numbers mean very little to me
25 years later they can still hear me
I left the womb
This is life

I steal so many kisses
I glance at your smile
Rosa the rose
Beautiful from the stem up
Rosa blossomed into nature
Nature of my love
The permanent smirk
I awake to new mornings
You by my side
My first kiss as the sun seeps in
My hug greeting you into your day
The car still runs
Your heart beats so slowly
I stare into your eyes
One more kiss,
Just one more kiss,
I want so many more

Sweet lover
This is more than enough
Let me take your hand on a journey
This distant planet I spoke of
Sunshine is forever bright
My hand will melt in your palm
Your heart has already melted
So did mine
You love me
I will never let go
This is us
Us is we
Come live with me

I sleep on many minds
I sleep very little
As I continue to make a move
They wonder how the cold days are
The nights of sitting alone
The summer days with not a worry
The words I speak of
The dreams I spew onto paper
The inexistent love I speak of
The man in the mirror
The back against the wall
Why I walk alone most times
This is me
I know no other way

Can my words save me or the people who listen?
I don't ride bicycles
Drive the fastest cars
Paint pictures like Michael Angelo
So who am I if you don't see me?
More than my words, I am
More than the stance I take
The sights I create
You see the words but not my eyes
I wish they could hear me speak
Listen to my tone
Watch me blur out
I am human just like them

Hold me, I get cold
Console me from the outside world
They can be so hateful
Leave the words outside
Let us sit in silence
Silence can be beauty
Close your eyes and see me
My eyes are closed as I envision
The first day we met
Love's stench fiddled its riddle
Say the words but before that
Take a deep breath and listen
I love you
I love you
Listen to the words
I love you

She called me a sky dreamer
A dreamer to an extent
Beyond the clouds my thoughts sit
As the wind blows them around
I search to capture them
Placing them in place
The place of where they collide
Concealed to conform
Objection is an option
Very little is left to decide
As I relay the emotion set forth
The play is set
The stage has been prepared
Listen to me
Listen to me

There comes a time in everyone's life
Where adversity is the only option
Death is the last option
Heaven or hell
Does it even exist?
The stories told before my time
The words they spoke of in my prime
I grew past the titles
He left before I even decided
The choices less to slim
I rode the bike on my own
I won in life
The bitterness had me secluded for some time
However I climbed the walls
The mountains humbled my existence
So when I speak listen
When I roar
It's not a bark
He sits in shame
This life created my smile

Again and again
Time has left its mark
As the seconds pass
They create the minutes
Creating the hours
Thus creating the days
The weeks and months
The years have passed
I have yet to stop this love that burns deep
Deep past my core
She has broken the lock
Thrown away the key
She is the last sip of the punch
Rosa's heart is the last if its kind
I love you
Simply put, I love you

My eyes remain blurry
As I can't foresee the future
For the past has left its stain
My mark is left unheard
My words appear oppressed
My thoughts are not buried
As my heart bleeds pain
I picture home in mind
This home of mine
I struggle to appear on the hearts
The minds leave me out
Again and again I keep coming back

Come home
Come back to where you were this morning
Dinner awaits your presence
It tastes better
My voice doesn't sound the same
Milo has separation anxiety from us together
His bark seems shallow
As he loves me
But loves us
Sleeping together he awakes us with a kiss
Between us he sits waiting to look
Deep with in us
Deep with in our eyes
As he knows destiny has put us together
Come home
Come home to Milo and me
We love you

I never fit in
I was born to stand out
Why play the role if I didn't fit the script
I changed the rules of engagement
They wrote what was supposed to be taught
I took it for what it's worth
I wrote my own words
It reflected what I was living
My lifestyle was unparalleled
I let my actions define me
My words are who I am

I wrote a poem for you
It told a short story
How I found you
How your eyes lit me up
Igniting a flame
Bursting into the air
Love's gush of support for you
Fireworks ablaze
You had not been at a place quite like this before
Stay close to the fire love,
Listen to the story
As I tell a tale about us
Tale of new beginnings
Journey with me to love
Love is love
This story of love
This story is love
Story of us

Since this is life
It is
What it is
The story behind it
Writing on the walls
Letters of something new
Out with the old
In with the new
Look at the colors
They shine bright
Clear as day
It appears for what it is
Since this is life
This is what it is

I'm releasing my words
Define the thoughts to mind
The complexity of the issues evolving
The nature of many events
Virginia Tech
London bombings
Far from Home
Pieces to a Dream
It was Written
Now this
I understand I can't feed the children
That, however, is not true
I can be the voice of reason
Sense of hope
The reason to dream
Nikki said bicycles
Because love requires trust and balance
I say love requires me
A love for everything

To my delight
To my sunshine
To my moon
To the stars
The gloomy clouds that hover over at midday
Take a deep breath
I took a glance
As I look on
I see love

Nikki Giovanni
Gave me food for thought
I created my own recipe
Thought provoking in every aspect
I gave it a go
She wrote the field notes
I made my own anecdote
Dinner at nine
I poured the wine
She herself prolific
I poised to be of greatness
Got a minute,
Take a walk with me
The blender sounds
She was yesterday
I am today
Tomorrow is left to create

Kevin Wright

I have circum to all the stereotypes
They depict me to be
What they want to see
My words have yet to be heard
The world awaits the silenced
I am unheard
Unread is my lisp
I spit when I speak
I came from afar
The distance seems too long
I continue to strive
Not to be like everyone else
To be elsewhere is evident
My words however
Seem always clear

I closed my eyes
Watched the sunset
Its existence quite clear
Revealing its intentions
Shining ever so bright
My dreams still glisten
Life remains at still
Travelling in my dreams
The sun moves away with me
Across the great sea
On the boat
Speed boats pass me by
I move at my own pace
Pouring love her wine
My eyes remain sky high
Love has such a sigh
I fit in here
This is where I belong
Beside love's side
Only in reality
I wish to appear

I sniffled when she walked in
I was cold
I saw love's vibrant smile
She walked past
To a walk back
I caught a glance of utter beauty
My words paused
I had not a thought, but a word
Beautiful
Creation at its best
Love's sincere eyes
I surrender
My heart and life
I surrender to serenity
Let the sky take us in
Home is where we are
Take me to the promised land
Love
Love is me

Tomorrow never promised
Today is life's gift
Love was here yesterday
The day before she just appeared
Shall I reveal myself to her?
My heart on my sleeve
My words of kindness
My thoughts not on paper
For them to leave my lips
Means taking a trip
Elsewhere to a distant planet
For perception is indirection
I am unlike the others
My love is beyond its existence
Beyond that kiss
Sense of touch
Love eludes me
What I see and hear
Music sings; the butterflies in my stomach
They fly and fly
Away into my heart
My soul to capture

I'm inspired by hate
Though to love
Anger is an emotion
As is love
Love can overcome an obstacle
Never leaving pain
Though behind in the back of the minds
Love shall conquer its prey
Thou shall love again
Love shall take its place
The garden still blooms
Love still and will forever gloom
Outside the box it's clear
Love will succeed

Wondering if you're listening
My heart beats for your existence
Take me in like the early sun
Walk with me in the forest
Let me spew my thoughts
You are my dreams
Do you know who you are?
You are love
You are my heart
My soul
Look straight ahead
Close your eyes
Let us sail into the sunset
The wind will see us through the storm
Past the rocks
Your hair is blowing
I just caught one of your kisses
Now feel mine love
This is love

The lyrics have changed
It's more consistent
The beat to her walk
Her smile more vibrant
The change in pace
The scent of its sense
Making no sense
Perfection seems impossible
I see it
She is for me
Love is for me

Let's trade shoes
See what I found by the lake
Beauty is an understatement
A rose blossomed over day
There it creped in my eyes
I watched it stand tall
Smiled at the sun
No rainbow in site
Only colors were the ones on our clothes
My eyes spoke vibrant thoughts
As my lips never moved
She knew what I meant by the looks of it
Body language and intuition
If she could read my mind
She would know
Know that love was in the wind
Wind to me by surprise
There I go
Away and away
Off into the sunset

They turn down the speakers
Before they knew I was there
Painted the walls black
Before they knew I existed
They turned off the lights
Before they could see my face
Lights out
Darkness it is
The painting on the walls
The graffiti that defines me
The words inscribed
The nature of my humanity
The injustice of my freedom of speech
They lost the hope
I hold the dreams
I held my dreams
In my hand
A grain of salt blew away
The dust never settled
Nor did my heart beat stop at a pace
The continuous motion
The trains never stopped to screech
The teary eyes of dead soldiers
My rants have me secluded
My word play makes me different
Mankind must not suffer
As I can breathe fresh air
Clean water has me on the hike to life
Dirty water speaks of such words
The lands that are lost
My words wish to sustain

Liability and ability are different
Ability of speech and word
I hold no crown in what I came to establish
A particular goal has me down a different lane
The lines I forbid to cross
I have crossed sometime ago
In the tunnels
Back out to the streets I scream peace for salvation
While the world seems at war
At war with my words
At peace with my thoughts
I chant 52 lines of power and heart
They see the vision
Others send a prayer
For this is worth what it is

In sleep I miss you
Your tender kiss
My tongue as it runs down your back
Back up your neck
As you turn over
I run back down
Stop at your luscious breasts
Right back downward
To your spot
I search for a pulse
I can make it beat
As I creep
Close your eyes
You inspire me on my search
Rubbing my head
Pulling me in deeper
As you run around and around
Circles are its pleasure
Side ridge sends volts
Let me drive
Rub down
Grip my ears
That's it love
That's it
Yes there
Climax love
Love climax

I found myself out from darkness
That dark road had its bumps and humps
I detoured into the desert
Sand blew
I never flew
For the sun shined elsewhere
Detours never in sight
Everything seemed the same
I walked and I walked
Alone in the present
Looking back on my past
The same seemed to follow
For it was the same
Love was something I couldn't remember
No clouds descending
No love pending
Clearness no clarity
Love is nowhere to be
I wish I could see love

Everything seems exception
A lot feels like deception
Weathering any given storm
How shall I reveal my thoughts?
My dreams are on paper
The world has yet to see my view
I'm everyday people
Normal like many
Different like the rest
Still driven by success
Rocks bottom
Has instilled its way
Refusing to bow in its presence
I am much more
I will give them more
More words
More food
I shall feed more hungry minds
Look in the sky
I am that sign

There I go in the rain
Showered with drops
Love continues to rain on me
I follow wherever it takes me
Past the stop signs
No limit past 40
Highway level of drive
Fast pace is love's heart beat
Switch lanes
Never letting go of the pedal
Speeding up and slowing down
Love still follows
Not behind, nor front
The star in the sky
Shall never leave us
Together and forever
Love is forever

I'm speaking for my city
For this city
On behalf of my city
In hopes to guide
In hopes the capture the essence
The one that died
Along with the past
I am the present
Failing am I not
I have grasped my own concepts
Failing not to transcend
For my words have failed to be read
The readers no exception
Non-readers missing out on
On what they can't read
Nor can they hear me
I want to roar
I wish I could clap for them
I can't
I won't
I wish on shooting stars
I am still here
Must I not preach?
For I've been put here to write
Read my words

I write
You listen
You read
I create pictures
You see
I paint imaginations
Instill the thoughts
Your dreams
My success
Stars float at night
Watch as they appear
Never as they seem
Dreams are what you make of them
They are yours
This is me

Never heard Jim Carrol speak
Never seen Emily Dickenson smile
Nikki Giovanni is super brilliant
Mona Lisa is a work of art
Art is love
Love is the passion they succeeded
Emotion, thought provoking
Let them live on

Broken promises
Sacred bonds broken
Love is pain
Pain is love
3 words leave its mark
I love you
Past time and endless fields
Happiness is that everlasting smile
Those tears of frustration and solitude
Confinement is that love bottled up
Bursting are the flames from the fire
Emotion is a crazy feeling
Pictures capture the moment
Snap shots are seconds in a lifetime
A kiss is everything and more
Hold please

Status is ever so evident
Love seems transparent
Words of wisdom
Dreams of hope
Preaching words of wisdom
The soul for it is to seek

Truth and love
The feeling of love
The truth and simplicity of it
The once was
Once upon a time
There she was
Here she is
Roses are bright as day
Beautiful as ever
She sleeps with a smile
The one I engraved
It remains permanent
I love you
So many words to tell you
I love you

Searching for a better
Better me
Better sense of existence
Displeasure is the many thoughts
My words are thought provoking
Cunning is my sense of direction
I produce hope for the directionally challenged
Wise beyond my years
Dreams are my existence
I write from inspiration
The clouds are my guidance
Love is my every support
Thank you love

Not sure if you can hear me
But dear love
Forgive me for my uncertainty
My insecure and fault
For I have never seen anyone like you
I have never been in love like this before
My past has me jaded
Deception is my direction
Searching for a new path
Trust is not my sane thought
Moving are the words of others
Speaking of things that don't matter
For a I feel like I'm a rock
Never can I be hurt
Image seems everything
It rains in my direction
I am no different
Rain drops hit me
I am human
I wonder if you'll ever betray me
I trust no one
Stubborn as I have always been
Hunger for love has always been my stench
Does she feel like I do?
Touch like touch?
Kiss me like I kiss her?
Love is my love

Kevin Wright

Whatever it is
This is something different
Unique yet not spiritual
The aura around me
I can feel it in the air
This is my world

She sits by the river
While the air blows through her hair
I remain at the window sill
Admiring beauty and sunlight collide
Is it more or am I dreaming?
I simply love you
You never leave my mind

Depression seems to be my struggle
State of mind
Mind in this existence
Existence in this life
Life appears out there in the clouds
No structure to follow
The lines not paved
The yellow line never to be crossed
Who created the boundaries?
The acts that follow
I never asked
Though I created my own
Disowning what they said
Abandoning the scriptures
This is who I am

25 years in the making
My words never cosigned
The rebuttals kept coming
Some wanted me to stop
Put the pen down
Ink to run out
As he left the house
The pain went with it
I started to wish
Brighter had to be created
My words instilled deep within in
Never could I rewind
I wish Nelson could give some of his time back
I wish I could create more
I wish on a lot
Hope for the best
Expect the worse
Life is
What we make it

They painted the walls black
Before I existed I saw the light
The clouds left a damp in sight
The dirt from the rain clouded my pores
Gasping for air
The words left me
The thoughts evaporated
I searched for what was left
As my dreams departed
I made the escape from reality
Reality never existed or did it?
My senses told me the script
I left it in that dark room
Never to be seen
Darkness surrounds me
Light appears dim with in
Struggling to exist

I'm not who I said I was
Who you wanted me to be
The vision you wanted to see
I am but him
The other side of things
Flip side of things to come
I have feelings
I do cry and sob
I am the hypocrite
I do get weak
The words simply hurt as well as uplift
I was left out in the dark
My heart drenched in shame
Forced to accept what it really was
Simply what it is

Poor before my demise
They may say those words
Rich I am for in this life I breath
Alone are the lost minds
Peace at mind the hearts around me
I remain secluded in my own realm
The clouds uplifting me
My presence remains at odds
Difference follows in my existence
I am that change

I've been in love
Nothing like this before
The fragrance is different
The taste of love is indifferent
Her smile is something new
Love's vibrant sense of life
Has me winded
Out of breath I am
I love love's charisma

I said I would never return
Love's heartbreak left me elsewhere
The roses smelled the same
The air wasn't purified
Bitterness filled the air
Life was as it appeared, a square
Everything sounded the same
Music spoke nothing
My walk was different
Confidence succeeded itself
I chose not to follow
My words meant something else
My thoughts died
I walked the opposite way
Until you showed up
Good morning breakfast
A dream just faded away

If this question I ache to be answered
Could be fulfilled-
Would the dreams stop?
Would love stop calling?
Would I feel indifferent?
Can I still be that missing thorn?
Can you answer questions?
Most important being…
Do you love me?
Like I love you…

The Jail cells see little daylight
I'm overshadowed by my shadow
It walks with me
While darkness thumps their walls
Imprisoned is my mind
Thoughts have me elsewhere
The water overtopping my head
Oxygen's short edge
Is it that I want?
Am I just like my people?
Freedom is not all it's cracked up to be, is it
Can I be this person who writes?
Can I be this person to uplift the jailhouse?
Succumbing the odds of survival
Never to be shackled
Bloodied or abused
Shackled by the very chains
Depression is a bitch
Success is bittersweet

Close the doors
Throw away the key
Keep away the negativity
Positive remains upstairs tied up
Let her not seep through the cracks in the walls
Release her words through the vents
Please fall on deaf ears
For that love I never want
Prison her existence
Must she not conform to what love is now
For it was something of not nature
But of something special
The lines remained straight
The rules changed
I through out the list
The past not forgotten
For the present is
The present wasn't
What it was before
The future seems beautiful
Prosperous are the remaining rocks
The waves still speak

Tomorrow remains a gift
Life has its shifts
The rhymes and riddles
The man on the corner still fiddles
My fist remains in the air
While the people around me stare
My eyes drenched in tears
For the many fears
I left something that was there
She still remains near
A lot of me died that day
So let what was there stay
She brings me back to it
My mind is foreign I know nothing
I pulled out the eraser
The tears on the pillow dried up long ago
The sky I left for you
The stars I spoke of to you
The stories I told you
The dreams I had
My existence and pleasures
I have to console
I found me

I miss you
I left you a message last night
I said I love you
I adore you
My loneliness leaves me without an existence
I knew love
Or did I?
The thoughts in my imagination
Want me to take you on a trip to the clouds
Where I live and look down on the world
Happiness up there exists
Down here is non-existent
You're at work as I leave this message
I know but I need you to know
I love you
Beep beep beep

Let's go
Come on lets go
Come on let's go and explore
Come on let's go and explore this new world

Love left her
Alcohol depressed her thoughts
Oppressed she didn't leave her mind
I wish I could be that change
The change she was hoping for
I have never left
Nor will I ever leave your side
You gave me life
Thank you

Come live with me
Listen to my alarm as it wakes me in the morning
Secure my smile
Kiss me on that rainy morning
Become my breakfast every morning

Just got your text
I smiled as I read your words
It said I love you
For some reason today
Yesterday
The day before
The same as the rest
Not the case
If I may make a case
I love you
Everyday is different
Everyday is brand new
Everyday is us
We
We are different

Made in the USA
Charleston, SC
03 July 2010